CLASSICS IN ACTION
KIDNAPPED

by Robert Louis Stevenson

Abridged by Brenda Ralph Lewis

Illustrated by Eric F. Rowe

Brimax Books · Newmarket · England

Introduction

Robert Louis Stevenson, novelist, essayist and poet, was born in Edinburgh in 1850. The son of a Scottish engineer, he spent most of his life plagued by ill-health and died in Samoa in the Pacific while still only in his forties. From his pen came *Kidnapped* – one of the most exciting historical adventures written in the English language. This, among his other novels full of suspense, action and realism such as *Treasure Island*, has enthralled generations of readers and takes a well-deserved place in classical literature.

The story is set in Stevenson's beloved Highlands of Scotland in the turbulent aftermath of the Jacobite rebellion in 1745. The Scots had suffered a bitter defeat at the hands of the English in the last great battle of Culloden. The cruel repression which followed caused unrest among the Scottish clans. Many rebels had been executed and thousands driven into exile.

Against this background, the hero, David Balfour, a quiet but determined youth becomes unknowingly heir to the great House of Shaws. His treacherous uncle, Ebenezer Balfour schemes to deprive him of his inheritance and David is kidnapped – a helpless captive aboard a slave ship bound for the Carolinas. His deliverance is aided by Alan Breck Stewart, a proud, flamboyant Scottish rebel. David finds in him a staunch friend.

They become involved with the death of Colin Campbell, the Red Fox, hated by the Scots because of his friendship with the English. Suspicion for his murder falls upon David and Alan. Then follows a series of wild adventures as in fear of their lives, they flee across Scotland pursued by their enemies.

Contents

ISBN 0 86112 772 2
Published by Brimax Books Ltd, Newmarket, England 1991.
Printed in Hong Kong.

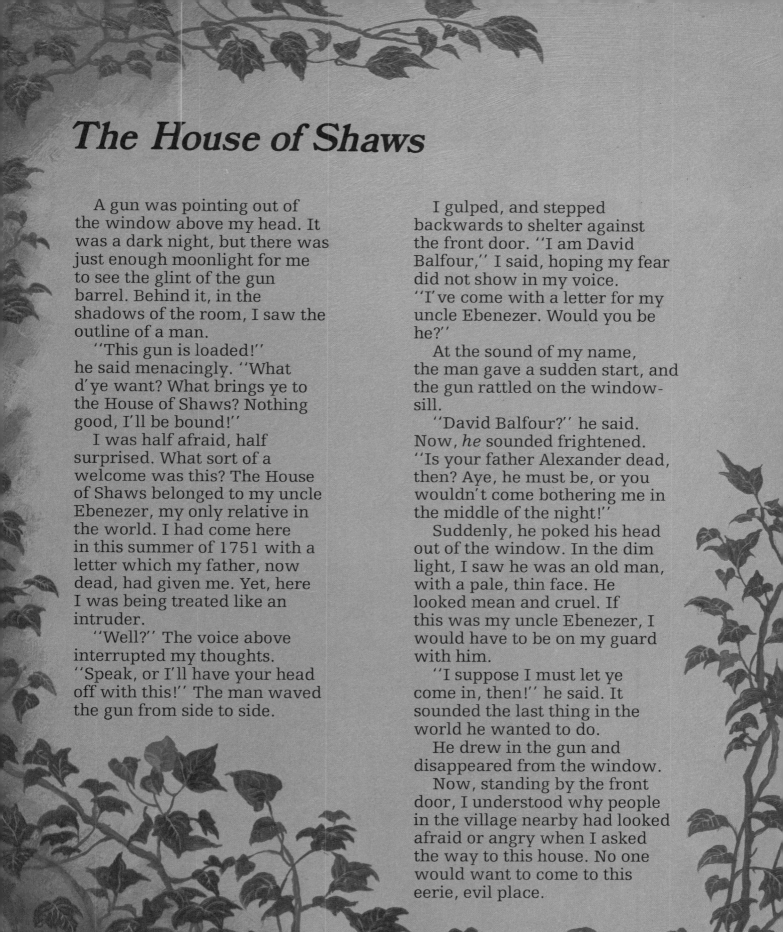

The House of Shaws

A gun was pointing out of the window above my head. It was a dark night, but there was just enough moonlight for me to see the glint of the gun barrel. Behind it, in the shadows of the room, I saw the outline of a man.

"This gun is loaded!" he said menacingly. "What d'ye want? What brings ye to the House of Shaws? Nothing good, I'll be bound!"

I was half afraid, half surprised. What sort of a welcome was this? The House of Shaws belonged to my uncle Ebenezer, my only relative in the world. I had come here in this summer of 1751 with a letter which my father, now dead, had given me. Yet, here I was being treated like an intruder.

"Well?" The voice above interrupted my thoughts. "Speak, or I'll have your head off with this!" The man waved the gun from side to side.

I gulped, and stepped backwards to shelter against the front door. "I am David Balfour," I said, hoping my fear did not show in my voice. "I've come with a letter for my uncle Ebenezer. Would you be he?"

At the sound of my name, the man gave a sudden start, and the gun rattled on the window-sill.

"David Balfour?" he said. Now, *he* sounded frightened. "Is your father Alexander dead, then? Aye, he must be, or you wouldn't come bothering me in the middle of the night!"

Suddenly, he poked his head out of the window. In the dim light, I saw he was an old man, with a pale, thin face. He looked mean and cruel. If this was my uncle Ebenezer, I would have to be on my guard with him.

"I suppose I must let ye come in, then!" he said. It sounded the last thing in the world he wanted to do.

He drew in the gun and disappeared from the window.

Now, standing by the front door, I understood why people in the village nearby had looked afraid or angry when I asked the way to this house. No one would want to come to this eerie, evil place.

Some villagers had even been unwilling to tell me where the house was. And one of them, an old woman, had cursed both the house and my uncle.

"When ye see that wicked man!" she cried "tell him Jennet Clouston curses him day and night. Tell him I'll dance with joy on the day of his death!"

I thought the old woman must be mad, or perhaps she was a witch. Now, I began to think there might be some good reason for her to hate the House of Shaws.

My thoughts were interrupted by the noise of bolts being pulled back. There was a rattling sound as chains were released. Then, with an eerie creak, the door opened and my uncle stood before me.

"Give me your letter!" he said, holding out a thin, bony hand.

"Will you not ask me in?" I replied, rather surprised.

My uncle frowned. "Oh, very well, come in," he said, reluctantly.

I stepped into a cold, dark entrance hall. "Go into the kitchen!" my uncle told me, pointing towards a half open door on the other side of the hall. "Don't touch anything, mind!" he added.

As I groped my way to the kitchen, I heard my uncle pushing the bolts and chains back into position on the front door. I felt like a prisoner, and even more so when uncle Ebenezer came in and locked the kitchen door too.

"So," he said, "so you are my younger brother's son, eh? How sad he should die before me, and me five years older!"

There was no look of sadness on his face as he spoke of my father's death, only meanness and greed. He was holding out his hand again. With great reluctance, I drew the letter from my jacket and gave it to him. His eyes darted back and forth along the handwritten lines. When he had finished, he smiled in a way that made me shiver.

"My brother has asked me to look after you, to see you come to no harm!" he said. "Well, perhaps I have some work for you. You're a strong lad, and I'm too old to be carrying the coals or sweeping floors . . . Well," uncle Ebenezer went on, "let's begin shall we?"

"Now? In the middle of the night?" I exclaimed in surprise.

"Why not?" he asked. "The night hours are as good as the day!"

Uncle Ebenezer reached into the pocket of his long, ragged gown and pulled out a rusty key. "Were," he said, "this is the key to the stair tower at the far end of the house. Go up the stairs and bring down the big chest at the top of it. There are some papers in it you should see.''

"Can I have a light?" I asked. "The stairway is dark, and there's a storm coming up."

I had heard distant rumbles of thunder while my uncle was reading my father's letter. Now, it seemed closer and already, rain was hammering against the windows.

To my astonishment, my uncle laughed. "You need no light, Davie," he said. "Just keep to the wall and you'll be all right!"

I must be mad, I thought, as I felt my way up the stairs. The wall was damp and cold; it was difficult not to slip on the uneven steps. At least, though, flashes of lightning occasionally lit the staircase and helped me climb. It was a long staircase, for the House of Shaws was five storeys high, but slowly, step by step, I made my way upwards.

I must have been climbing for ten minutes when a crash of thunder startled me and made me stop and cling to the wall. A brilliant fork of lightning flashed through a nearby window, blinding me for a moment. But out of my half open eyes, I thought I saw something strange about the stair two or three steps ahead. I lowered myself slowly until I was lying on my front and extended my arms as far as they would go. I could feel the first step was solidly made. The second tipped a little, but would have taken my weight had I stepped on it. But the third! I felt round it, and my fingers closed upon a jagged edge of stone, with nothing beyond it.

To make sure, I heaved myself up on my elbows and felt the step again. I was right! The staircase came to a sudden end. Without that flash of lightning, I would certainly have fallen over the edge.

It could only mean one thing: my uncle had tried to kill me.

I started to tremble with shock, but at length, this was replaced by anger at my uncle's wickedness. Silently, I swore I would get my revenge.

Carefully, I groped my way down the stairs. About half way down, a glimmer of light from the kitchen showed me a man standing in the rain, as if listening. Suddenly, lightning flashed. It was uncle Ebenezer! Another crash of thunder and my uncle jumped with fear and scuttled back into the house. I crept down the rest of the stairs and followed him through the kitchen door. He was sitting at the table with a bottle of brandy in front of him. Now and again, he shuddered and groaned, then gulped a mouthful of brandy.

Suddenly, I stepped forward and clapped both hands down upon his shoulders.

"Gotcha!" I cried.

Uncle Ebenezer gave a cry, flung up his arms and tumbled to the floor like a dead man. For a moment I wondered what I should do. I knew that first, I should get some sort of protection before my uncle recovered. He had failed once to kill me, but he would certainly try again.

After a short search, I found a dagger in a large chest, and hid it inside my waistcoat.

My uncle still lay as he had fallen, all huddled up. I was frightened that he might be dead, so I threw some water in his face. To my relief, his eyes opened. When he saw me, a look of terror crossed his thin face.

"Are you alive?" he sobbed. "Oh, Davie, are you alive?"

"I am," I replied grimly. "Small thanks to you!"

He clutched his throat. "The blue phial," he gasped, breathlessly. "In the small cupboard . . ."

I ran to the cupboard and found a blue medicine phial.

I gave my uncle a dose from it and he seemed to recover. "It's my heart, Davie, my heart!" he murmured pitifully.

I hoisted him into a chair. He looked very sick, and I felt a moment of pity. But I was also furious, and started firing angry questions at him. What did he mean by sending me into such danger? Why had he tried to kill me?

Uncle Ebenezer listened in silence. Then, he begged me to help him to bed. "I'll tell ye in the morning," he said in a sorrowful voice.

He was so weak, I had to agree. Once he was in his room however, I locked the door and put the key in my pocket.

Kidnapped at Queensferry

Next morning, I watched my uncle as he ate his breakfast and satisfied myself that he was well enough for a man-to-man talk.

"Well, sir," said I, firmly. "What have you to say? Why do you fear me? I can think of no other reason for your sending me to my death!"

Uncle Ebenezer muttered something about liking a bit of fun, but I was sure he was preparing some new lie or trick.

I was just about to say so when there was a knock at the front door. When I opened it, I found standing before me a young boy dressed in sailor's clothes. The poor fellow was blue with cold.

"I've brought a letter from old Heasy-oasy for Mr Ebenezer Balfour!" he said cheekily, and pulled it from his shirt.

The letter was signed by Elias Hoseason — or "Heasy-oasy" as the little fellow called him. It was written from the Hawes Inn at the Queensferry. In it, Captain Hoseason asked whether my uncle had any further commands, seeing his ship would soon be sailing.

"You see, Davie," my uncle explained, "I have some business with this man Hoseason. He's captain of a trading brig, the 'Covenant'." He nodded towards our visitor who, it seemed, was Hoseason's cabin boy. "If you and me was to walk over with yon lad, I could see Hoseason at the Hawes Inn or maybe on board ship. After that, we could see Mr Rankeillor, my lawyer. He knew your father — a very respectable man is Mr Rankeillor!"

I wondered if my uncle had another trap in mind for me, but decided that I would be safe among all those ships and people down at the docks.

"Very well," I said at length. "Let us go to the Ferry."

As we trudged towards Queensferry, the cabin boy, whose name was Ransome, talked about Captain Hoseason, and his Chief Officer, Mr Shuan. Shuan, who drank a great deal, seemed a cruel brute. Ransome showed me a raw, red wound on his leg, and said, as though proud of it, "Mr Shuan done that . . . he done that!"

With such cruelty occurring on board, I began to think the 'Covenant' must be a hell upon the seas. All the more so because, as Ransome told me, she carried criminals to America to work as slaves on the tobacco plantations.

At last, we reached the top of the hill and looked down at the Firth of Forth, and the town of Queensferry.

"That's the 'Covenant'!" said Ransome pointing to a ship lying at anchor. I looked on it with great dislike.

"I shall not go on board," I told my uncle firmly.

Uncle Ebenezer, who had said nothing since we left the house, seemed to waken from a dream. "Eh?" he said. "What did ye say?"

I told him again, and he said "Well, well! Ye need not, if ye don't want to!"

We walked down to the town, and came to the Hawes Inn. Ransome led us upstairs to a small room, where a dark, serious-looking man sat writing at a table near a blazing fire.

"I'm fair pleased to see you, Mr Balfour!" he said in a deep voice, offering his hand to Ebenezer.

"My word, Captain, you keep this room uncommonly hot," my uncle replied, fanning his face with his hat.

He was right. The heat of the room was making me feel drowsy. So, although I had resolved not to let my uncle out of my sight, I went outside to get some fresh air. Ransome followed and asked hopefully if I would buy him a bowl of punch.

"You're far too young to drink punch," I replied, "but you may have a glass of ale."

We went into the inn together, and were soon sitting at a table. There I got into conversation with the landlord.

"Did you come with old Ebenezer?" the landlord wanted to know.

"Yes," I replied.

"You'll be no relation of

his?'' he asked, suspiciously.

I did not like the sound of this. ''No, no relative,'' I lied.

''I thought not,'' the landlord answered, seeming relieved.

The landlord had no liking for my uncle — that was clear.

''Is Ebenezer not liked around here?'' I asked.

''He is not!'' said the landlord firmly. ''He's a wicked old man! There's many who'd like to see him hanging at the end of a rope!'' The landlord leaned across, as if to whisper some secret.

''Ebenezer was a fine young fellow once,'' he informed me. ''Then, people started to gossip about how he'd killed his brother, Alexander. He turned very nasty after that!''

I was horrified. My uncle killed my father? What terrible talk was this?

''Why? Why did he kill him?'' I asked, trying not to show how shocked I was.

''To get the house, of course — the House of Shaws!'' was the reply.

''Is this true?'' I gasped. ''Was my . . .'' I nearly said 'father' but stopped myself. ''Was Alexander the eldest son, then?''

''Indeed he was!'' the landlord answered. ''Why else would Ebenezer kill him?''

So, I thought, the House of Shaws was my rightful inheritance from my dead father. It was a grand thought, though I was still appalled at what the landlord had told me.

Just then I heard my uncle calling me. He was standing outside the inn with Captain Hoseason.

''Mr Balfour tells me great things of you,'' said Hoseason.

"For my part, I've taken quite a liking to you. Perhaps you'd care to come aboard ship and drink a bowl of punch with me!"

This sounded suspicious. I sensed danger.

"But what about going to Mr Rankeillor?" I asked, hoping this would serve as an excuse to refuse the Captain's invitation.

But to my dismay, Hoseason said: "You can go by boat from the 'Covenant' to a pier in the town, not far from Mr Rankeillor's house!"

Suddenly, Hoseason leaned down and whispered: "Be wary of this wicked old uncle of yours, he means mischief. Come aboard so I can speak with you!"

With that, he put his arm through mine, and went on in a loud voice: "What can I bring you from America, my lad? We voyage to the Carolinas — there are many fine things there." All the while, he was walking with me towards his boat. As he helped me climb in, I felt the Captain was a good friend, and suspected nothing. Not until I was hoisted on board, to find my uncle was nowhere to be seen, did I start to become afraid.

"Where is Mr Balfour?" I demanded.

At once, the Captain's friendly manner changed. Now he looked grim and menacing.

"It's no use asking for him, lad!" he said. "He won't help you!"

I had been tricked! I fought to escape the Captain's grasp and ran towards the side of the ship, only to see the boat pulling away. My uncle was sitting in its stern.

"Help! Help!" I cried. "Save me!"

My cry echoed round the harbour. Hearing it, my uncle turned and I saw on his face a frightful look of cruelty.

Suddenly, strong hands dragged me back from the ship's side. Then, a thunderbolt seemed to strike me. I saw a great flash of fire, and everything went dark.

Murder!

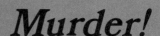

When I came to my senses, I was in darkness. My head ached intolerably, and I was tied hand and foot. All round me there was the roaring of water, and the thundering of the wind. One moment, the ship was heaving upwards. The next, it was rushing downwards. I felt so confused that it was some time before I realised I was below decks in the 'Covenant'.

Obviously, she was caught in a violent gale.

I dozed, then woke, then dozed again. How much time passed I cannot tell, but all at once I was wakened by a light. A man was standing nearby, holding a lantern. He was about 30 years of age, not very tall and in the dim light, I saw he had a mop of fair curly hair and green eyes.

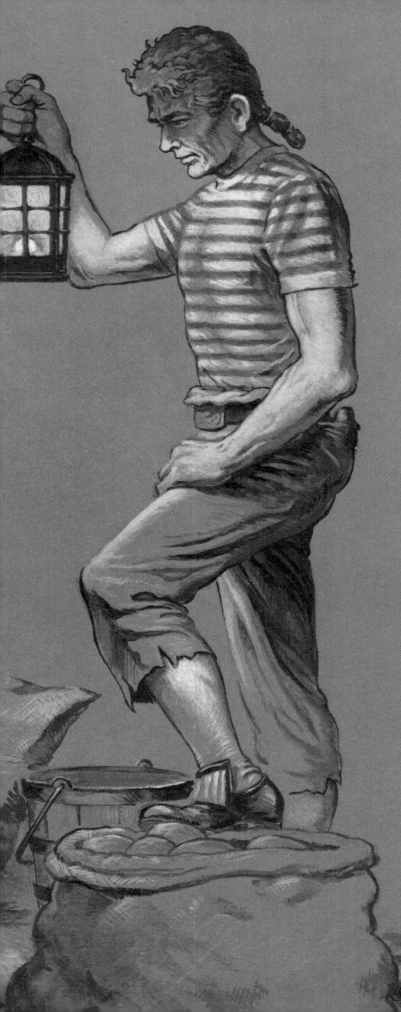

"Well," he said, looking down at me. "How are you feeling?"

I answered with a groan. The man felt my forehead, then set about washing the wound on my head, where, I presumed, I had been struck with something hard.

"The wound's not so bad," he said comfortingly. "Have you had anything to eat?"

"I don't want anything," I groaned.

He gave me some brandy and water, then left.

Next time he came, Captain Hoseason was with him. I felt so ill that I had no idea how many hours had gone by since his first visit. Hoseason stood looking at me, frowning.

"You see for yourself, sir," the seaman told him. "The boy has a fever! He's eaten nothing! He must be taken out of this hole!"

"No, Mr Riach!" Hoseason replied grimly. "Here he is, here he shall stay!" With that, the Captain made to leave, but Riach caught him by the sleeve.

"You were paid by that wretch Ebenezer to murder this boy!" he accused.

Hoseason turned on him. "What's that?" he cried. "What did you say?"

"A murder — you were paid to do a murder!" Riach repeated.

Hoseason was clearly worried by Riach's accusations.

You say the lad will die if he remains here . . .'' he said slowly.

''Aye, he will!''

The Captain hesitated, then gave in.

''Do as you please, Mr Riach!'' he said angrily.

The ropes that bound me were cut. I was carried up into the forecastle, laid in a bunk and covered with blankets. After a while, as I began to recover, I started noticing the men who came in and out of the forecastle. They were a rough lot, but very talkative. Some told me how they had once been pirates. Others were criminals or deserters from the Royal Navy.

The cabin boy Ransome came to see me from time to time, and I was distressed to see he had new wounds. Once, he had a very badly bruised arm, and told me that it was Mr Shuan, the Chief Officer, who had done it.

Then, one night, a seaman came to the forecastle with terrible news.

''Mr Shuan has done for him at last!'' he whispered. Something dreadful must have happened to Ransome, I thought. I became certain of it when Captain Hoseason came to see me.

''Well, my man,'' he said kindly. ''We have a job for you! You'll serve in the roundhouse and wait at table instead of Ransome!'' I was surprised, and hesitated. ''Come on, lad!'' cried the Captain. ''Get up to the roundhouse, and set to work!''

Just then, two seamen appeared, carrying Ransome in their arms. Ransome's face was white as wax. My blood ran cold.

''Go on!'' the Captain told me again. ''Get to work!''

I jumped up, fearfully, brushed past the two sailors, and ran up the ladder onto the deck.

The roundhouse was a good sized room. There was a table and bench fixed to the floor and two bunks. One was for the captain, the other for Shuan and Riach, who slept in it in turn.

A tall, black-haired man sat at the table, with a brandy bottle in front of him. He was powerfully built, and had an evil, cruel-tempered look. This, I supposed, was Shuan. He was very drunk and took no notice when I entered. Soon afterwards, the Captain came in.

''How is poor Ransome?'' I whispered to the Captain.

He said nothing, just shook his head gravely.

Just then, Riach entered. He and the Captain exchanged serious glances. I knew what it meant: Ransome was dead. For a moment, no one moved. Then, Shuan reached out to take the brandy bottle, but Riach snatched it away.

''You've had enough of this, you brute!'' Riach cried.

At once, Shuan jumped to his feet.

"'Sit down!" the Captain roared. "You drunken swine, you've murdered the boy!"

Shuan sat down, and buried his face in his hands. "Well, he brought me a dirty cup!" he said in a trembling voice.

At this, the Captain sighed, and led Shuan to his bunk.

"Get some sleep, man!" he said sadly.

Shuan began to cry, but he lay down, as the Captain had ordered.

"This must never be known on shore!" the Captain muttered to Riach. "The boy went overboard — that's our story!"

My duties in the roundhouse involved serving meals and drinks, but being unaccustomed to such work, I did it clumsily. Sometimes, I fell while carrying plates or glasses and spilled everything over the floor. But Riach and Hoseason were very patient with me. I expect it was because of what had happened to Ransome.

More than a week went by and it seemed that the ship made no headway against the strong sea winds. Three days later, we were surrounded by thick, white fog, so thick that you could not see one end of the ship from the other.

At about ten o'clock that night, the ship gave a great jolt. At once, Hoseason and Riach leaped to their feet.

''She's struck the rocks!'' Riach cried.

''No,'' the Captain told him. ''More like we've run down a small boat!''

They hurried out on deck. The Captain was right. We had run down a boat in the fog, splitting it in two. Of the men on board, only one survived and then only by amazing luck and unusual strength. When the 'Covenant' struck, he leaped up, caught hold of the ship's bowsprit and so saved himself.

He was a smallish man, with a sunburnt complexion and a skin pitted with smallpox scars. His eyes were very light and had a look of daring in them. When the Captain brought him into the roundhouse and he took off his greatcoat, he laid a pair of fine silver mounted pistols on the table. I saw there was a great sword at his waist. He seemed a sturdy, dashing fellow.

Hoseason looked him up and down, rather suspiciously. ''So,'' he said, ''you've a French soldier's coat on your back, and you speak with a Scots tongue!''

''Ah, are you then of the Jacobite party, Captain?'' the man asked, referring to the supporters of Bonnie Prince Charlie, the Stewart claimant to the Throne.

The Captain replied that he was no Catholic Jacobite, but a true-blue Protestant. That meant that he was loyal to the Protestant King of England, George II. The Scots Jacobites had rebelled against King George in 1745, but their rebellion failed, when they suffered a crushing defeat at Culloden in 1746. Afterwards, the Scots had been made to suffer cruelly. Their land was taken from them, and they were forbidden to wear their native tartan dress. About eighty rebels were executed, and thousands more driven into exile. From what our visitor said next, it seemed as if he

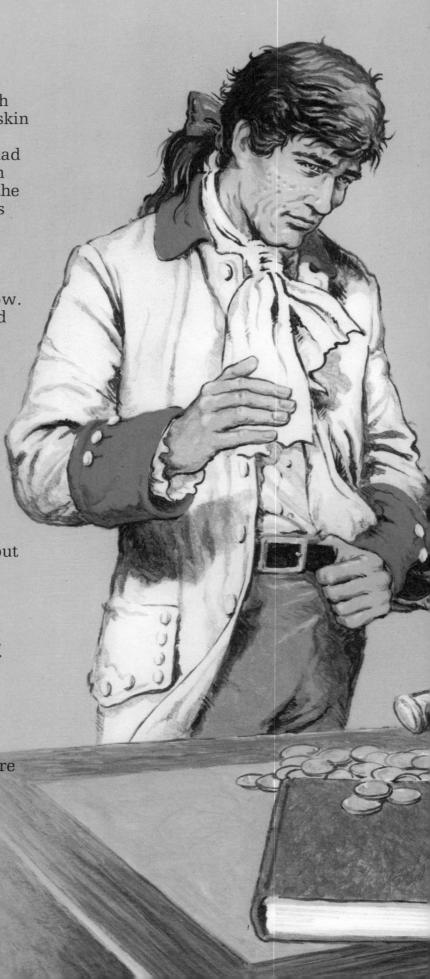

was one of these unfortunate fugitives.

"I was making for France, sir," he told Hoseason. "A French ship should have picked me up, but I missed it in the fog. Still, if you could take me there, I could reward you well!"

"That I cannot do," Hoseason answered. "I could set you back on the Scots shore, though . . ."

Just then, Captain Hoseason sent me to the galley-kitchen to fetch some supper for the Jacobite. When I came back,

the Jacobite had poured some coins onto the table.

"Thirty guineas if you set me on shore, Captain — sixty if you set me on Linnhe Loch . . ." he was saying.

Hoseason was tempted. "Sixty guineas — and the bargain's made!" he said. "Here's my hand upon it!"

The battle of the Roundhouse

Soon afterwards, the Captain hurried off and left me with the stranger.

"So you're a Jacobite," I said, as I set some meat before him.

"Aye," he answered. "And you, by the look of your long face, would be one of those Whigs loyal to King George!"

He guessed correctly, but I had no wish to annoy him. "Betwixt and between", I replied. "Neither for King George, nor against".

"Well, Mr Betwixt and Between," he replied. "This brandy bottle is empty. If I am to part with sixty guineas, I think I should have decent drink!"

I said I would fetch him fresh drink, and went on deck to ask the Captain for the key to the cupboard. He was talking to Riach and Shuan, and it looked to me as if they were up to no good.

"If we persuaded him to come on deck, we could get him then," Riach was saying.

"No," returned Hoseason. "Suppose we get him talking, one of us on either side of him. We can grab his arms then and take him prisoner!"

I felt hot with fury. These treacherous, greedy men were plotting against the Jacobite! I must help him —

and all at once, it occurred to me how I could do so.

"Captain!" I said, approaching him. "The gentleman has asked for more drink. Can I have the key?"

They all jumped at the sound of my voice. Then, a cunning look came onto Riach's face.

"Our firearms are in the roundhouse," he said. "Here's our chance to get hold of them! Davie — d'you know where the pistols are?"

"Aye, he knows," Hoseason told him, putting an arm about my shoulders. "Davie's a good lad," he grinned. "You see, that Jacobite there is a danger to the ship and a sworn foe of King George, God bless him. We need our firearms to defend ourselves against him. Will you get them for us? If you do, you'll have your fingers on the gold he carries in his money belt!"

I felt disgusted, but told the Captain I would do as he wished.

The Captain gave me the key to the drinks cupboard. I fetched a bottle and hastened back to the roundhouse.

"Do you want to be killed?" I said. The Jacobite sprang to his feet in alarm. "They're murderers here!" I continued. "They've killed one boy already.

Now they plan to kill you!''

"Do they?'' the Jacobite cried. "Well, they haven't got me yet! Will you stand by me lad?''

"That I will! I am no murderer!''

The Jacobite smiled. "What's your name?''

"David Balfour,'' I replied. Then, remembering that despite my present plight, I was a man of property, I added: "Balfour of Shaws!''

"My name is Stewart,'' he told me proudly. "Alan Breck, they call me.''

There was no time for more talk. We had to look to our defences. The roundhouse was strongly built, with two stout oak doors. One was already shut, and I locked it. I was just about to lock the other, when Alan Breck stopped me.

"Leave it open,'' he instructed. "When my enemies come in, they'll find me facing them!''

Alan went over to the rack that held the ship's weapons. He handed me a cutlass, a powder horn, a bag of bullets and all the pistols, and told me to load them.

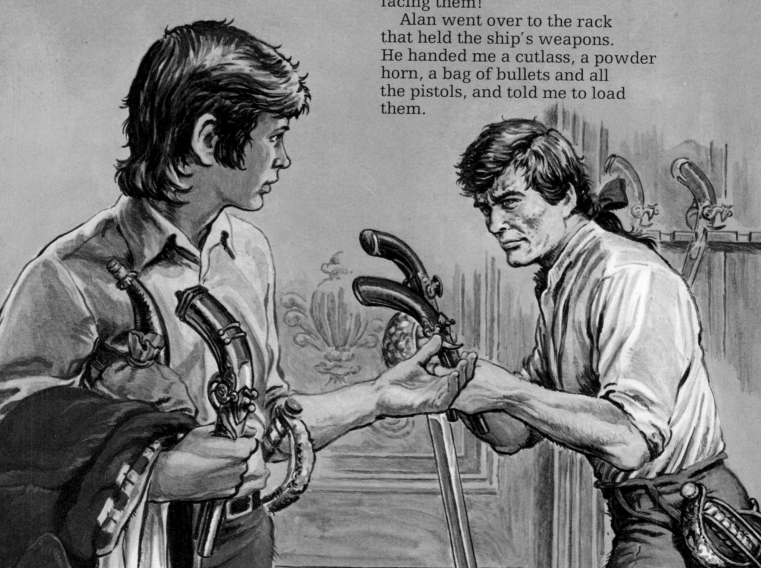

I was excited, and frightened at the same time. Two of us against so many attackers! There were at least fifteen of them, and when I told him, Alan whistled in alarm.

"Well, that can't be cured," he said. "Now, here's my plan of battle. I'll defend this open door. You keep watch on the other, in case they break it open. They might come through the skylight, too," said Alan, looking up at the small window set in the ceiling of the roundhouse.

"How can I watch two places at once?"

"You have ears, haven't you?" Alan replied.

"Of course!" I cried. "If they come through the skylight, I'll hear glass breaking."

By this time, Hoseason was becoming impatient. Several minutes had passed, and I had not returned with the firearms. Suddenly, Hoseason appeared at the door and Alan pointed his sword at him.

"A naked sword!" cried the Captain. "A strange return for my hospitality."

"I know you've been plotting, Captain!" Alan said defiantly. "Let's get on with it — call those louts of yours, and get a taste of good Stewart steel!"

The Captain glared at me, with an ugly look on his face. "Davie," he growled. "I'll remember your treachery!"

Next moment, he was gone.

"Keep a cool head, Davie," Alan told me encouragingly.

Alan drew his dagger, and held it in his left hand, while his right hand gripped his sword. I climbed into one of the bunks with an armful of pistols and looked out of the window onto the deck, keeping watch for attackers. The sea had quietened down, and the wind was steady, so I could hear the muttering of voices, and then the scraping of steel. They were handing out the cutlasses!

All of a sudden, there was a rush of feet and voices roaring. I heard Alan shout. I looked over my shoulder and saw Shuan in the doorway, crossing swords with him.

"He killed the boy Ransome!" I shouted.

"Keep watch at the window!" Alan yelled, and as I turned back to do so, I saw his sword pass through Shuan's body.

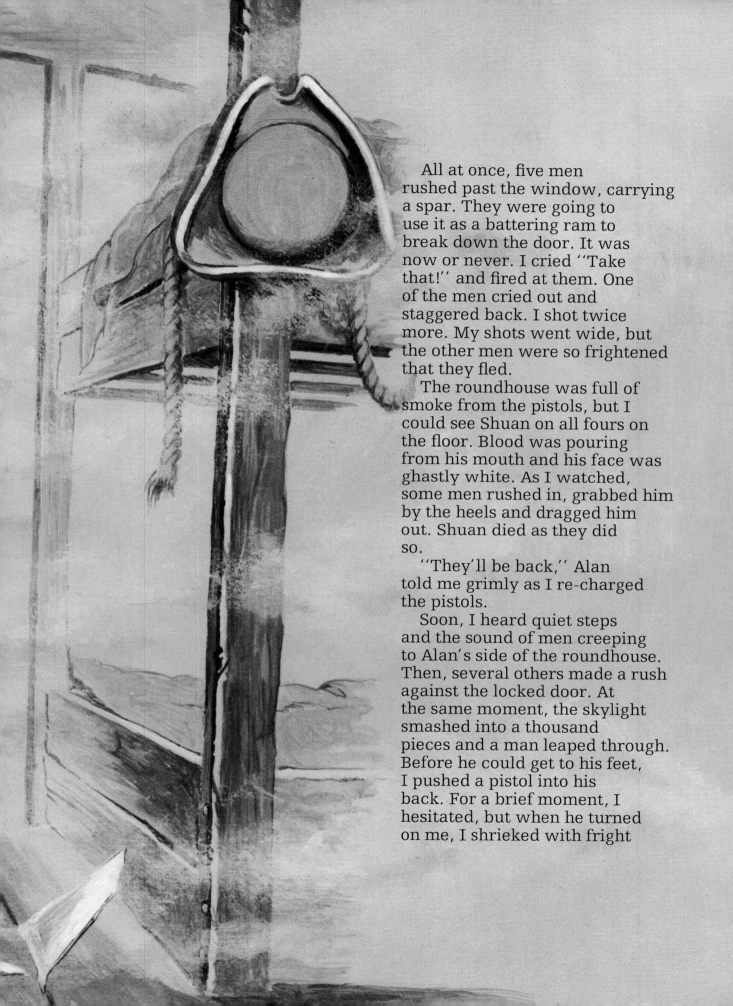

All at once, five men rushed past the window, carrying a spar. They were going to use it as a battering ram to break down the door. It was now or never. I cried ''Take that!'' and fired at them. One of the men cried out and staggered back. I shot twice more. My shots went wide, but the other men were so frightened that they fled.

The roundhouse was full of smoke from the pistols, but I could see Shuan on all fours on the floor. Blood was pouring from his mouth and his face was ghastly white. As I watched, some men rushed in, grabbed him by the heels and dragged him out. Shuan died as they did so.

''They'll be back,'' Alan told me grimly as I re-charged the pistols.

Soon, I heard quiet steps and the sound of men creeping to Alan's side of the roundhouse. Then, several others made a rush against the locked door. At the same moment, the skylight smashed into a thousand pieces and a man leaped through. Before he could get to his feet, I pushed a pistol into his back. For a brief moment, I hesitated, but when he turned on me, I shrieked with fright and fired. The man fell down with a horrible groan, just as another fellow, whose legs were dangling through the skylight, kicked me in the head. I snatched up another pistol and shot at him. He tumbled through the skylight and fell in a heap.

I stood, stunned, but a shout brought me to my senses. One of the attackers had ducked under Alan's sword and though Alan was striking at him with his dagger, the fellow clung round his waist like a leech. There were more armed men behind him. As I grabbed my cutlass and rushed to help Alan, he managed to shake off the man clinging round his waist, then ran towards the others, his sword in front of him. They took fright, and ran, falling over each other in their haste. Alan charged onto the deck, and drove them before him as if he were a dog chasing sheep.

When he returned, Alan was elated.

"Davie, my boy!" he cried. "Am I not a bonny fighter?"

My reaction to our victory was quite different. I felt terrible at the thought of the killing I had done, and began to cry like a child. Alan put a comforting hand on my shoulder. "You're a brave lad, Davie," he said. "Get some sleep and you'll feel better!"

Shipwreck!

All night, Alan and I took turns to keep watch in case the attackers returned.

As the hours passed, Alan and I became fast friends. He cut off one of the silver buttons on his coat and gave it to me as a keepsake.

"Show that button and friends of Alan Breck will help you wherever you go!" he told me.

After breakfast next morning, I heard Riach calling from the deck. I climbed through the broken skylight and pointed a pistol at him.

"The Captain wants to speak to your friend," he said wearily.

"How do we know he means no treachery?" I replied.

Riach shook his head. "No Davie," he said. "To tell you the truth, the men wouldn't follow him if he wanted to make another attack."

Alan agreed to a parley, and when Hoseason came to speak with him, it was clear the ship was in trouble. She had drifted close to the Isle of Mull, and the few men fit enough to work the ship did not know this dangerous coast.

"I'll have to put back to Glasgow and take on more men," Hoseason told Alan.

This was no good to Alan, and though Hoseason argued and pleaded, he had to agree in the end to keep to his bargain and set Alan ashore in his own country. Of course, Alan could not pilot the ship to a safe landfall, but, he told Hoseason, he had been picked up and set down on this coast often enough to know something about it.

The Captain had to be content with that, and in return for a bottle of brandy, let us have two buckets of water to wash the blood of battle off the roundhouse floor.

That done, Alan and I sat talking and smoking, while he told me something about himself. He led a dangerous life, for he was wanted by the English as a rebel. Yet, every year, he journeyed secretly to Scotland to collect the rents due to the exiled chief of his clan, Ardshiel of Appin. James of the Glens, Ardshiel's half-brother, collected the money and Alan took it back to Ardshiel in France.

"It's hard for those tenants," Alan sighed. "They have to pay rents to King George as well!"

"That is very noble — to pay two lots of rent," I said.

"Aye, it's noble indeed!" Alan replied. "They're fine folk, with staunch spirits and they're true to their chief!

They may be poor, these folk, but they don't grudge a second rent for the sake of Ardshiel — even though they may go hungry for it!''

As he spoke of the sacrifice these people made, and the hardships they suffered, Alan's eyes glistened with tears. Suddenly, a look of fury crossed his face.

''If the Red Fox ever hears of it,'' Alan muttered fiercely, ''he'll gnash his teeth to pieces!''

I guessed, from Alan's expression and the harsh tone of his voice, that the Red Fox was a deadly enemy.

''The Red Fox? Who is he?'' I wanted to know. Alan looked grimmer than ever.

''Why, the wickedest villain in Scotland!'' he replied. ''It was the Red Fox — Colin Campbell of Glenure is his name — who grabbed Ardshiel's lands after the English had driven Ardshiel away . . . Oh, the greedy, black-hearted devil! One day, I'll get my revenge on him — be sure of that!''

Late that night, Captain Hoseason put his head round the door. He looked anxious. ''Come and see if you can guide us,'' he said to Alan.

When we came on deck, the 'Covenant' was tearing through the sea at a great rate, pitching and tossing. A low roaring noise sounded across the turbulent moonlit waters.

''It's the sea breaking on a reef,'' Hoseason said gloomily. ''I know not how we're going to get past safely . . .''

''Captain — I think these will be what they call the Torran Rocks,'' said Alan. ''They stretch for about ten miles. I've an idea that the way through lies close to the Isle of Mull.''

Hoseason seemed relieved. ''All right, Mr Riach,'' he said to his officer. ''We'll come into shore as near to Mull as she'll go.''

He turned to Alan. ''Pray God you're right!'' he said grimly.

''Pray God I am!'' Alan whispered to me.

Nearer and nearer the ship came towards the rocks. Every now and again, Riach shouted from the rigging where he was keeping watch, telling the steersman to change course.

It was extremely dangerous. The 'Covenant' sheered to one side or the other to avoid a rock, and when she came alongside Mull she hit a strong tide which threw her about.

Then, to our relief, Riach yelled ''Clear water ahead!''

''You've saved the ship, sir,'' Hoseason told Alan gratefully. ''You were right about the way through the rocks!''

The Captain spoke too soon, for the tide suddenly seized the ship, and spun her round like a top. Next moment, she struck the reef with such force that we were all thrown flat onto the deck. When I scrambled up, the wind was thundering and shrieking in the ship's sails and huge waves were pouring down upon the decks.

Some of us tried to launch the skiff into the raging sea. As we struggled and strained, Hoseason stood by, stunned by what had happened. Every time the ship hammered on the rocks, he groaned, for he knew the merciless reef was destroying her.

As for Alan, he was looking very worried. I looked across to the shore, and asked him what land this was. ''The worst possible,'' he answered. ''The land of the Campbells — the land of my greatest foe, the Red Fox!''

All at once, a tremendous sea seized the 'Covenant', lifted her up and shoved her over onto her beam end. I was thrown clean overboard, hurled about and several times thrust under the sea before I found myself in calm water, floating with the help of a spar.

Fortunately, the shores of a small isle, called Earraid, were near enough for me to reach. I waded ashore, exhausted, but very grateful for my escape. It was half past midnight, and so cold that I dared not sit down, in case I froze to death. Instead I walked to and fro trying to get warm. At daybreak, I climbed the hill in the centre of Earraid and looked around. There was no sign of the 'Covenant' or the skiff, no sail to be seen at sea, and on the isle, not a single house.

This was the start of four days of fear and suffering. I recall them now with shame, as well as with horror. For it would never have happened had I not been so ignorant of the tides and the sea. I had thought there was no way to get off the island by myself. I fancied I would have to wait for a boat to take me across to the Isle of Mull. So, I waited and waited, getting more and more hungry and miserable, as the rain poured down without ceasing. Day after day, it rained, until it seemed there was not one single dry spot on the whole of Earraid. I even had to sleep with my clothes clinging, soaking wet, about me, and my feet immersed in a bog.

Drenched and wretched as I was, I made things even worse when I tried to stop my hunger pangs by eating some shellfish. Shellfish seemed to be the only food I could find, but no sooner had it passed my lips than I was seized with giddiness, pain and retching. The pains were like sharp spears. I felt so bad that after the first attacks passed, I lay for a long time feeling more dead than alive.

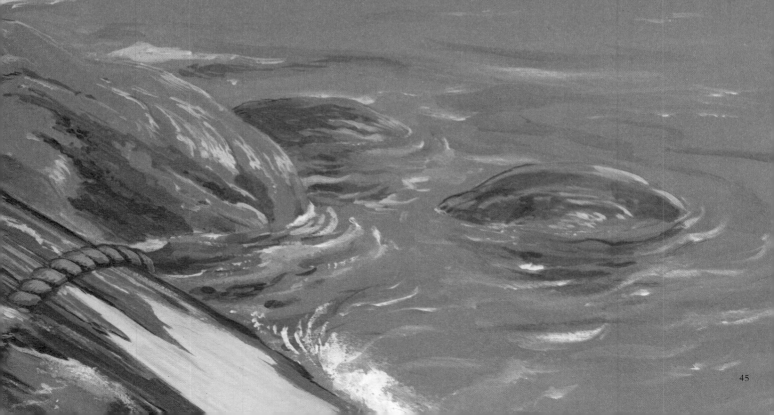

Two days went by in this miserable fashion, and I began to believe I was doomed. Never again would I see a warm fire or know the comfort of human company. Then, suddenly, on the third morning, I saw a boat not far off. Greatly excited, even a bit hysterical, I started shouting and waving to attract attention. The two men in the boat certainly heard me. Yet, to my horror, they took one look at my bedraggled figure, then started laughing and sailed on past the island! I could not believe my eyes. Such cruelty! Such inhumanity! I burst into a wild sobbing. I screamed. I tore at the turf until my hands bled. Over and over again, I cursed the two men for their wickedness, and prayed they would die some dreadful death for leaving me stranded.

All the same, on the fourth day, I kept a lookout in case they returned. Imagine my joy when they did, indeed, appear, in the same boat. Imagine my embarrassment when they told me that when the tide was out, the water in the creek was so low, I could have waded across to the Isle of Mull!

I dashed down to the creek. The water was only knee-deep! A few minutes later, I was on the Isle of Mull, feeling very grateful to those two fishermen whom I had previously cursed. If they had not troubled to come back, then I could have died on Earraid, and left my bones there for ever.

The murder of the Red Fox

The Isle of Mull was rugged and trackless. The only landmark I knew was some smoke I had seen while I was on Earraid. I made my way in that direction and at last came upon a house, in the bottom of a hollow. An old man was sitting outside, smoking his pipe. I was relieved to learn from him that my shipmates had managed to get ashore safely.

Naturally, I was most anxious to know about Alan. "To be sure," the old man said, "one of the men wore breeches like a gentleman. The others wore sailors' trousers."

Then, he clapped his hand to his head as if he had suddenly remembered something.

"Would you be the lad with the silver button?" he asked.

"Why, yes!" I replied.

"I've a message for you. You're to follow your friend to his country, by way of Torosay."

Four days later, with one hundred miles of hard tramping behind me, I found myself on board a ferryboat, crossing the Sound of Mull from Torosay to the island of Morven. The skipper of the ferryboat was called Neil Roy Macrob, and he was a member of the same clan as Alan Breck Stewart. I had to wait until we landed on Morven, at Kinlochaline, before I managed to get Neil Roy to one side. At first, he was suspicious of me, but when I showed him Alan's silver button, he became more friendly.

"I've been told to make sure that the lad with the silver button is safe," he said. He had also been told to pass on Alan's instructions for guiding me to the house of James of the Glens. Before we parted, though, Neil Roy had a warning for me.

"Don't speak to anyone," he cautioned, "particularly not a Campbell. Avoid red-coat English soldiers and never, never mention the name of Alan Breck Stewart! It would be better if you forgot you ever knew it!"

These were grim words indeed, and I soon discovered why, for my travelling companion next day was a man who seemed to know all about the Stewarts and their great enemies, the Campbells. My companion's name was Mr Henderland, a small, stout fellow who was a minister of religion. It was Mr Henderland, not I, who mentioned Alan Breck.

"He's a bold, desperate fellow is that Alan Breck," Mr Henderland told me. "He'd stop at nothing — not even murder!"

I was rather shocked to hear this, and shocked, too,

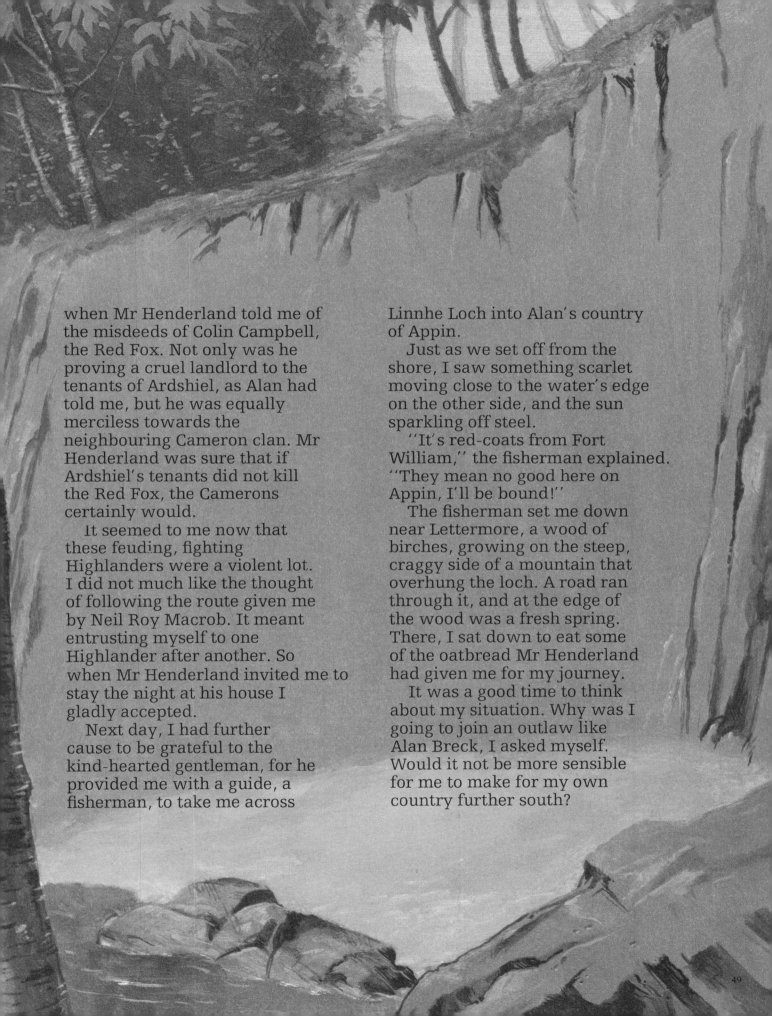

when Mr Henderland told me of the misdeeds of Colin Campbell, the Red Fox. Not only was he proving a cruel landlord to the tenants of Ardshiel, as Alan had told me, but he was equally merciless towards the neighbouring Cameron clan. Mr Henderland was sure that if Ardshiel's tenants did not kill the Red Fox, the Camerons certainly would.

It seemed to me now that these feuding, fighting Highlanders were a violent lot. I did not much like the thought of following the route given me by Neil Roy Macrob. It meant entrusting myself to one Highlander after another. So when Mr Henderland invited me to stay the night at his house I gladly accepted.

Next day, I had further cause to be grateful to the kind-hearted gentleman, for he provided me with a guide, a fisherman, to take me across Linnhe Loch into Alan's country of Appin.

Just as we set off from the shore, I saw something scarlet moving close to the water's edge on the other side, and the sun sparkling off steel.

''It's red-coats from Fort William,'' the fisherman explained. ''They mean no good here on Appin, I'll be bound!''

The fisherman set me down near Lettermore, a wood of birches, growing on the steep, craggy side of a mountain that overhung the loch. A road ran through it, and at the edge of the wood was a fresh spring. There, I sat down to eat some of the oatbread Mr Henderland had given me for my journey.

It was a good time to think about my situation. Why was I going to join an outlaw like Alan Breck, I asked myself. Would it not be more sensible for me to make for my own country further south?

While I was trying to make up my mind, I heard the sound of horses. Soon afterwards, four travellers came around a turn in the narrow path. The man in front was a red-headed fellow with a proud, commanding look about him.

By now, I had decided to go on with my adventure and make for the house of James of the Glens as Alan wanted. When the travellers came closer, I asked the red-headed man the way to Aucharn, where James' house lay. He seemed to think that this was amusing. However, the man behind him, a gloomy-looking lawyer, commented rather brusquely: "Glenure, this is no time for jesting!"

Glenure! I thought with a sudden shiver. This red-headed man was none other than Colin Campbell, the Red Fox.

He was glowering at me. "And what d'ye seek in Aucharn?" he asked.

"The man who lives there."

"Ah, James of the Glens," said the Red Fox thoughtfully. "Why do you seek him? I should tell you, I have power here and many soldiers hereabouts supporting me."

It was time, I thought, to make my loyalties clear.

"I am an honest subject of King George," I declared.

The Red Fox had been looking at me rather doubtfully, but my words seemed to set his mind at rest.

All of a sudden, the sound of a gunshot cracked out from higher up the hill. At once, the Red Fox tumbled from his saddle onto the road.

"They've killed me," he groaned. As the lawyer held him in his arms, and his servant stood over him, the Red Fox looked from one to the other.

"Take care of yourselves," he murmured weakly.

Then the Red Fox gave a great sigh and his head rolled to one side. He was dead.

The lawyer seemed struck dumb. His face had gone white. The servant burst out crying, and I stood staring at them all, horrorstruck. The fourth man, a sheriff's officer, ran back along the path, to fetch the soldiers.

As the lawyer laid the Red Fox down on the road, in a pool of his own blood, the movement brought me out of my shock. I started scrambling up the hill and suddenly spotted a big man wearing a black coat with metal buttons. He carried a long-barrelled gun.

"Here!" I yelled. "I see him!"

At that, the murderer looked quickly over his shoulder and ran faster. For a while he was lost to sight, but then I saw him again on the other side of the woods, climbing quickly up the mountainside.

Beneath me, on the path, the lawyer and the sheriff's officer were shouting and waving. Red-coated soldiers, armed with muskets, appeared out of the woods below and to my horror, I heard the lawyer yell: "Ten pounds if you capture that lad! He was posted to hold us in talk — he's an accomplice to the murder!"

I was so amazed, that I remained helpless where I stood. Even when the soldiers began to spread out, some running, others pointing their guns at me, I was still unable to move.

Then, a voice jerked me out of my helplessness.

"In here, among the trees," it said.

Hardly knowing what I was doing, I obeyed. As I did so, I heard guns firing and musket-shot come whistling through the branches.

Inside the shelter of the trees, I found none other than Alan Breck. He was holding a fishing rod.

"Come!" said Alan.

He set off running along the side of the mountain and,

Alan recovered first. "Well," he said, "that was a fine burst of speed, Davie!"

I said nothing. I was thinking that I had seen a murder done and the man killed was the one Alan hated most in the world, and here I found Alan skulking among the trees and running away from the red-coats. Was Alan the murderer? The thought so horrified me that I could not look him in the face.

"Are you all right?" Alan asked, realising something was wrong. "Alan," I burst out suddenly, "we must part — your ways are not God's ways!"

"I can hardly part from you without reason," he answered gravely. "If you know some thing against me, let me know of it!"

"You know very well the Red Fox lies dead down there . . ." I began.

I had more or less called Alan a murderer and he regarded me sternly.

"First of all, Mr Balfour of Shaws," Alan said, "I would not kill anyone in my own country, to bring trouble on my clan. What's more, I could not kill any man with a fishing rod which is all I carry now."

Alan took his dagger from his belt and placed his hand upon it. "I swear that I had neither part, nor act, nor thought in that murder!" he said solemnly.

"Thank God for that!" I cried, and offered him my hand.

like a sheep, I followed him. We kept on and on, sometimes ducking behind rocks or crawling on all fours through the heather. Every now and then, Alan straightened up and looked back the way we had come. Every time the pursuing soldiers saw him and started shouting and yelling.

After about fifteen minutes, Alan turned round, and sped back across the mountain-side until at last we reached the same place where I had found him. We were both panting hard and I had a pain in my side.

"But do you know who did it?"

"He came very close to me to be sure, but by amazing coincidence, I just happened to be tying my shoes at the time."

Alan meant, I supposed, that he wasn't going to give away a man who had killed the great enemy of his clan. As I knew, Alan had even tried to draw the attention of the soldiers to himself, so that the murderer could escape.

Now, though, Alan grew very serious. "With the Red Fox dead, Appin will be searched from top to bottom," he told me. "We've both been seen around here and that's enough to make the red-coats think us guilty!"

"Where shall we go?"

"To the Lowlands," was Alan's answer. I liked the idea for I was very anxious to get back to my home there.

"Right," said Alan. "Let's go and see what the red-coats are doing". We looked down between the birchwood trees and saw the red-coats in the distance. They looked like toy soldiers.

"Thank the Lord," I breathed. "They've lost us!"

"Aye," said Alan. "After we've eaten and rested, then we'll strike out for the house of James of the Glens. There we'll collect my clothes and my weapons, and a bit of money. Then, my lad, it's the Lowlands for us and safety!"

On the run from the Red-coats

When night fell, we were still tramping the rough mountainsides, with the cloud-filled sky black and sinister above our heads. It was about half-past ten when we reached the top of a hillside where, below us, we saw lights. There seemed to be people moving around, outside a house, carrying lighted torches.

Alan gave a signal — three whistles — to reassure the people below that we were friends.

We were met at the gate of the house by a tall, handsome man of about fifty.

"James of the Glens!" Alan greeted him. He put his arm through mine. "This young fellow is a gentleman of the Lowlands, but it'll be better for his safety if we don't mention his name."

James greeted me courteously, but then turned to Alan with a worried look on his face.

"It's dreadful," he said, and wrung his hands.

"Hoots, man!" Alan replied. "The Red Fox is dead — be thankful!"

"Aye," said James gloomily. "And I wish he was alive again. Mark my words, the people of Appin will pay for this murder!"

All round us, I saw anxious-looking people taking guns, and other weapons from their hiding places in the house and farm buildings, and burying them further down the hill.

"If the English red-coats were to find weapons here, we'd all be doomed!" James explained, sounding very worried.

While Alan went off to change into the clothes James was keeping for him, James took me into the kitchen. He was smiling and pleasant at first. However, he soon grew gloomy and sat frowning and biting his fingers.

James's wife sat near the fire, weeping, while his son

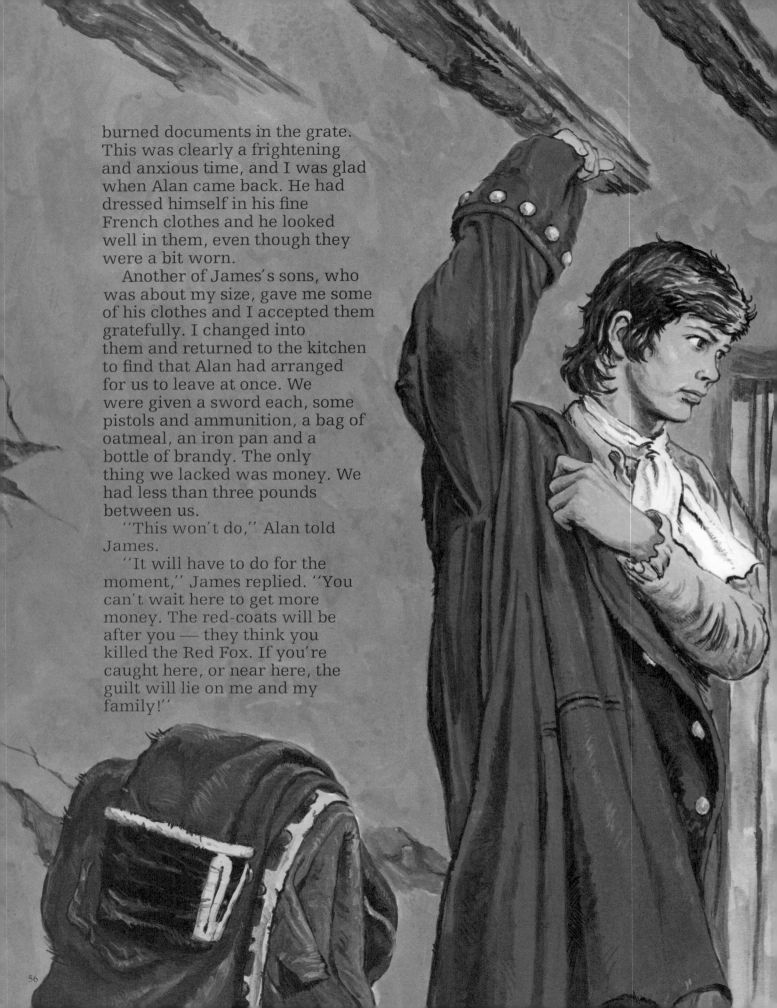

burned documents in the grate. This was clearly a frightening and anxious time, and I was glad when Alan came back. He had dressed himself in his fine French clothes and he looked well in them, even though they were a bit worn.

Another of James's sons, who was about my size, gave me some of his clothes and I accepted them gratefully. I changed into them and returned to the kitchen to find that Alan had arranged for us to leave at once. We were given a sword each, some pistols and ammunition, a bag of oatmeal, an iron pan and a bottle of brandy. The only thing we lacked was money. We had less than three pounds between us.

"This won't do," Alan told James.

"It will have to do for the moment," James replied. "You can't wait here to get more money. The red-coats will be after you — they think you killed the Red Fox. If you're caught here, or near here, the guilt will lie on me and my family!"

All at once, James seized Alan by the front of his coat. "Get away, Alan, you and your friend — get away as fast as you can!" he cried earnestly. "You must understand . . ." he went on haltingly. "I'll have to make out that I'm helping the red-coats find the Red Fox's murderer! You know what that means, don't you?"

Alan's expression was very grim now, but he said nothing.

"It means I'll have to agree to putting a price on your head, Alan — yours and your friend's!" James went on. "If I don't . . ." James broke off, trembling. "It'd be a dreadful thing if I were to hang . . ." he finished, lamely.

"Aye," Alan said in a low, sad voice. "Aye, James, I understand your position . . ."

The more I heard of all this, the more appalled I grew. Why not simply tell the red-coats the name of the man who had, in fact, killed the Red Fox? Then, honest, innocent folk like myself could show their faces in safety. When I tried to explain my feelings, though, Alan and James cried out in horror, bidding me to hold my tongue.

"What would the Camerons think if we did such a thing?" they protested. From that, I presumed that the murderer was a member of that clan. But I could see it was no use trying to argue any further — the strange feuds and alliances of these Highland clans were completely foreign to me.

Although I detested the idea of having a price on my head when I was guilty of nothing, there was not much I could do about it. I was already a fugitive, after all. So, I put the best face I could on the matter, and at last, Alan and I said farewell to James and went on our way.

We travelled all night and at dawn found ourselves in a rock-strewn valley. There was a foaming river running through it and wild mountains on either side.

"This is not a safe place," Alan frowned. "The red-coats are bound to watch it!"

Alan ran down to the waterside, to where the thundering waters of the river leapt so high that a mist of spray hung above it. Three rocks stood in the middle of the river at this point, and with a great leap Alan landed on the middle one. He fell to his hands and knees to stop himself slipping off. I followed, and Alan caught me. I was overcome with fear and put my hand over my eyes, shuddering violently. Alan started shouting at me, but I could not hear, so great was the noise of the river. The next minute, Alan put a brandy bottle to my lips, forcing me to drink a great mouthful.

Then, he turned and jumped across the water to land safely on the opposite shore. I was now alone on the rock. Well, I thought, if the red-coats catch me, I will hang, and if I fall into the river, I will drown. Not much of a choice.

So, I bent my knees low and flung myself forward. My hands clutched at the river bank, then slipped, but luckily Alan seized me and lugged me onto the bank beside him.

We started running again, until we came upon two huge rocks, some twenty feet high. After several tries, we managed to climb to the top, where we found a large hollow. From here, we could see the valley and the river, but nowhere the smoke of a house or any living creature.

"Get some sleep," Alan told me. "I'll keep watch."

I slept until about nine o'clock when I was roughly awakened. I opened my eyes to find Alan looking very worried.

I soon saw the reason for Alan's anxiety. The red-coats had arrived. Some were in a camp half a mile from the river and along the riverside there were sentries. Higher up, we could see men on horses riding to and fro.

"If they get up the sides of the hill, they can spot us with a spy-glass," Alan whispered.

If the red-coats kept to the lower part of the valley, we could be safe, and when night came, perhaps we could try to get past the sentries down by the river. There were not so many of them there.

We passed a terrible day.
The sun beat down, making the
rock too burning to touch. We
had no water, only some brandy.
At least, though, we managed to
keep the brandy bottle cool by
burying it in some peat that had
settled on top of the rock. So
we got some relief, but not much,
by dabbing cool brandy on our
foreheads and chests.

All day, we watched the
soldiers patrolling and hunting
among the rocks. Some of them
shoved the ends of their pikes
into the heather: if we had
been hiding there . . . I
shuddered to think what would
have happened to us. Some of
the soldiers came close to the
base of the rocks on which we
lay. We hardly dared breathe
in case they heard us.

So the day passed, and as
the tedious hours went by, the
intense heat made us feel
dreadfully dizzy. We got
fierce pains in our arms and
legs. I felt as if I was
frying. Then, at long last,
a small shadow fell on the
east side of our rock about
two o'clock in the afternoon.
Thank goodness it was out of
sight of the red-coats! Moving
as quietly as we could, Alan and
I slipped over the edge of the

hollow and gratefully dropped down into the shade. We stayed there, still sick, giddy and aching for an hour or two. If the red-coats had come upon us, then we would have had no strength to try to escape. But, fortunately, none came and no red-coats spotted us from further off.

After we began to recover Alan suggested that we make our getaway. Moving as quietly as we could, we slipped from one rock to another, sometimes crawling flat on our bellies, and gradually drawing away from where the soldiers were. By sunset, we had moved a fair distance.

We came upon a fast-moving stream, a wonderful welcome sight. Straight away, we plunged head and shoulders into the cool, foaming water and drank our fill. It was marvellously refreshing. We rested there next day, setting off again at nightfall. We scrambled up the steep mountainsides with the loch far below us, shining in the moonlight.

Our destination was the Heugh of Corrynakiegh, a cleft at the top of a great mountain with a shallow cave in the rock close to some running water. It was still dark when we reached it. It was a beautiful place, full of birch trees and, further on, a pinewood. On one side stood the country of Mamore, on the other, the country of Appin.

In a low, concealed place we made a fire and cooked some porridge and grilled the trout we caught in the stream.

''We'll be safe here for a while,'' Alan murmured, ''but we must send word to James to get some money to us.''

How could we send word to anyone, from this wild, deserted place, I wondered. But Alan had the answer.

''Lend me that silver button I gave you, Davie,'' he asked.

Alan fashioned a cross from a piece of wood and blackened the ends in the fire. Then, he strung the silver button on a strip of cloth from his great coat and tied sprigs of birch and fir to it.

''There is a little hamlet not far from here called Koalisnacoan,'' Alan said when he had finished. ''My good friend, John Breck Maccoll, lives there. When it gets dark, I will steal down and put this cross on his windowsill.''

I was mystified. ''But what will that tell him?''

''That Alan Breck Stewart is hereabouts and needs help,'' Alan explained. ''The silver button will tell him my identity, and the sprigs of birch and fir will show him we are up here!''

''Why not write him a message?'' I asked.

''He can neither read nor write! This is the only sort of message he will understand!''

The Quarrel

That night, Alan slipped down to Koalisnacoan and put the cross on John Breck's windowsill. Next day, at about noon, we saw a man struggling up the mountainside towards us. Alan, recognising him, gave a few whistles to guide him to where we lay.

I did not like the look of John Breck Maccoll. He seemed dull-witted and unpleasant, and when Alan asked him, he refused to take a verbal message to James.

"I'll carry a letter for you" John Maccoll growled, "or leave you here to rot!"

Alan found a dove-quill in the wood, made some ink from gunpowder and water and then tore the corner from a letter which he carried in his pocket.

"Dear Kinsman," Alan wrote. "Please send money by John Maccoll to the place he knows of, Your affectionate cousin A.S."

John Maccoll did not return for three days. With him, he brought a letter from the wife of James of the Glens, and five guineas which was all she could scrape together — and some very bad news.

James, his wife wrote, was in prison in Fort William, together with some of his servants.

"So!" I thought, "James did *not* convince the English that he meant to help them solve the murder of the Red Fox!"

However, one part of James's plan had succeeded — and only too well. The English had offered one hundred pounds for Alan's capture and mine. That was obvious from the handbills describing the two of us which James's wife sent with her letter. As I read the handbills, it crossed my mind that I would be better off without Alan, for if I were caught with him, an accused murderer, the consequences could be very serious. But I felt rather ashamed at the thought, and said nothing.

There was nothing to do but press on. We left Corrynakiegh and marched through the mountains all night before coming to a stretch of broken moorland. This was dangerous country for it was flat and offered few hiding places from the red-coats.

Still, we had no choice, so we set out across the moor until, at about noon, we lay down to rest and sleep under a heather bush.

It was here that we came very close to disaster.

We took turns to keep watch but it was so hot that I dozed

off when I should have been
looking out for red-coats.
Suddenly, I woke up with a
start, to find to my horror,
some red-coat cavalry nearby.

In great panic I shook
Alan awake.

"What are we to do now?"
I asked, frightened and ashamed.

"We'll make for Ben Alder,"

Alan whispered, pointing to a
mountain that lay to the
northeast. "We can hide
there."

"That will take us across
the path of the red-coats!"

"I know, but we have to
take the risk. Come on,
Davie — quickly!"

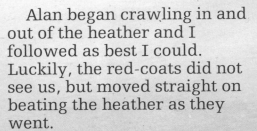

Alan began crawling in and out of the heather and I followed as best I could. Luckily, the red-coats did not see us, but moved straight on beating the heather as they went.

We kept on, both of us panting with effort, our hands and knees scraped and sore.

Even when it grew dark and we saw the red-coats making their camp, we went on crawling and stumbling through the heather. I grew so weary that by the time the next day dawned, it seemed as if years had passed. But we were out of the worst danger by then. By that time, we were staggering along, utterly exhausted. We were going down a hill when suddenly three or four men leaped at us out of the heather. Next moment, Alan and I were lying on our backs, each of us with a dagger at his throat.

I was too tired to be afraid. Then, I heard Alan whispering something in

Gaelic and the daggers were taken from our throats.

"What luck!" Alan told me. "These are Cluny's men — we could hardly have fallen into better hands."

I thought the fugitive Jacobite, Cluny MacPherson, was in France. Yet here he was, still in Scotland! What was more, he was only too glad to give us shelter. I was very relieved at this, for as Cluny's men led us to his mountain hideout nearby, I was feeling very lightheaded and dizzy.

By the time we reached the hideout — 'Cluny's Cage' on Ben Alder — I had to be carried in.

Cluny MacPherson greeted us warmly.

"Well, well, if it isn't Alan Breck!" he smiled, puffing on an evil-smelling pipe. "Come in, come in!"

Alan introduced me as the Laird of Shaws, which made me feel rather grand.

I felt a little better after drinking some brandy which Cluny offered us, but when we sat down to a meal, I could not eat very much.

Afterwards, all I wanted to do was sleep, and I had hardly put my head down on a bed of heather in one corner of the cave before I dozed off. I seemed to be in a trance for a long time. I kept hearing men talking, and saw shadows moving on the mud walls of the 'Cage'. Once, I looked over to where Alan and Cluny were playing cards. I saw a pile of one hundred guineas or so on the table. Next, I remember Alan coming over and asking me to lend him money. I had been brought up to believe cards and gambling were ungentlemanly, but I felt so ill that I handed over the money without argument. My fever took two days to pass, but as we prepared to resume our journey, I got a dreadful shock.

"Davie," Alan confessed miserably, "I've gambled all our money away!"

"All our money?" I gasped, horrified.

"All of it," Alan groaned.

Cluny insisted on giving the money back, but I was so furious with Alan that I refused to speak to him.

That night, Alan and I were rowed across Loch Errocht and set down on the eastern shore. From there, we were led to another of Cluny's hiding places by a gillie who carried all our baggage. I remained silent the whole way. After a while, Alan could bear it no longer, and tried to get me into conversation. He wanted to apologise but I would not let him and lapsed again into furious silence.

Towards evening next day, Cluny's gillie took us across Loch Rannoch and told us the best way to take to make good our escape.

It was not a welcome route, for it ran through Campbell country. But there were few red-coats there, or so the gillie assured us.

This was by far the worst part of our journey, and not just because there was such bad feeling between Alan and myself. It rained without ceasing as we crossed eerie mountains and skirted wild rivers.

I was constantly cold, so cold that my teeth chattered, and I started to feel ill again.

To make me even more miserable, I was feeling angry with myself because I could not yet find it in my heart to forgive Alan. He kept offering to help me, but though I needed help badly, I kept on refusing. At last, Alan seemed to decide he had been made to suffer enough.

He began to walk jauntily, instead of plodding along, and kept whistling songs and teasing me for being a Whig and loyal to King George. This made things worse, for my anger with Alan built up so much that at length we nearly came to blows. It happened when Alan taunted me with the nickname "Whiggie!" just once too often. Ill as I was and feeling dreadfully sick, I felt I must have it out with him once and for all.

"Mr Stewart," I cried, trying to stop my voice quivering. "Henceforth, you shall speak civilly of King George!"

"I am a Stewart," Alan started to say, but I interrupted him.

"Oh yes," I jeered. "I know you bear a king's name. But in the Highlands I have seen a good many others who bear it — and they would be none the worse for a good bath!"

"You insult me, sir," Alan said in a low, trembling voice.

"I am as ready as yourself," I replied defiantly.

"Ready?"

"Come on!" I cried, drawing my sword.

Alan was appalled.

"David!" he cried. "Are you daft? It would be murder if I were to draw my sword against you!"

"That was your lookout when you insulted me!" I replied.

For a moment, Alan stood perplexed. Then, he shouted: "You speak true, Davie!" and drew his sword. But before his blade could touch mine, he threw his sword down. "No, no," he murmured. "I cannot, I cannot!"

All at once, my anger disappeared. I felt terribly ashamed of myself. I had wronged Alan when he had been so kind and courageous. At the same time, I was feeling horribly sick and there was a pain in my side like a sword thrust.

"Oh, Alan!" I wept. "Forgive my bad temper — if you don't help me, I will die here!"

"Don't say that, Davie, don't say that!" Alan was nearly in tears. "Let me get my arm about you," he continued. "Now lean upon me . . ."

As he propped me up, he was almost sobbing out loud. "Oh, Davie," Alan sighed. "I'm no right man at all. I have neither sense nor kindness! It's you who'll have to try to forgive me!"

"Let's say no more about it," I gasped.

"Be of good cheer, Davie — we're in Balquhidder now," Alan told me. "We'll find shelter there!"

Safety at Last!

It was risky for Alan to knock at any door in Balquhidder, for many of the clansmen there were no friends of the Stewarts. Fortunately, the first house we came to belonged to a man who knew of Alan and respected him. His name was Duncan Dhu Maclaren.

For a whole month Duncan and his wife tended and sheltered me until I was once more well enough to take to the road.

With the passing of so many weeks, Alan thought that the hunt for us must have lost its first urgency. So he suggested that we journey towards the Lowlands by way of the Firth of Forth, and its chief crossing point, the Stirling Bridge.

"No one will expect us there," Alan explained. "It's good policy to go where you're least expected."

Three days later, after a surprisingly easy walk to Stirling, we lay close to the high, narrow bridge along the parapet. This was the way to safety and I was so excited that I wanted to cross the bridge at once. Alan stopped me.

"It's too quiet for my liking," he said.

So, we waited until we saw an old woman approach. She started across the bridge, but after she had gone a little way, we heard a voice cry:

"Who goes there?"

A musket rattled. There was a sentry on duty!

"This'll no do for us!" Alan muttered. "We'll have to try to get across by boat somewhere further down."

Very disappointed, we tramped off eastwards, until next morning we reached a hamlet called Limekilns.

Across the water lay Queensferry. It was a heartwarming, but also a heartbreaking, sight, for I could only gaze on it, still not knowing how I was going to get across there.

But I reckoned without Alan and his cunning. It all started when we bought some bread and cheese from a kind-looking lass at an inn in Limekilns.

As we sat eating our food in a small wood nearby, Alan was thinking.

"That lass could get us a boat, Davie!" he said at last.

"How?" I wondered, thoroughly puzzled.

"A bit of play acting," Alan replied and winked at me.

A few minutes later, I was stumbling back into the inn, with one arm round Alan's neck. He was half-carrying me.

"The poor lad's walked hundreds of miles!" Alan explained to the startled lass, and softly whistled a few bars of the Jacobite song 'Charlie is my Darling'.

"Well, well," the lass murmured, thinking, as Alan had wanted, that we were Jacobites on the run.

"Well, unless we can escape . . ." said Alan, and struck the back of his neck, meaning we would lose our heads.

The lass, who was obviously sorry for us, gave us some food, then sat looking at us. She was troubled and when Alan asked her to help us, she shook her head in fright.

"No, no, I couldn't!" she protested.

"Now look here, my lass," said Alan. "I saw two boats down on the beach just now. All we want is someone to row us across the Forth, and keep quiet about it afterwards!"

The lass made no reply. Perhaps a touch of the truth might persuade her, I thought.

"Did you ever hear of Mr Rankeillor?" I asked.

"Mr Rankeillor the lawyer?" she exclaimed. "Why, yes! A good man — everyone knows that!"

"Well," I told her, "I'm on my way to his house, so you see I'm no evil-doer."

The lass looked relieved. "Well, that's all right, then," she said. "I'll find some way to get you across the water!"

She told us to hide in the small wood by the waterside until she sent word.

At about eleven o'clock, we heard the sound of oars. We looked out, and saw the lass herself rowing towards us.

"We must be quick!" she urged.

It took only a short time to row to the south shore, where she set us down. The lass shook hands with us and straight

afterwards began rowing back towards Limekilns.

"She's a fine lass, a very fine lass," Alan murmured gratefully.

At last, I was back on my home ground and out of danger. Alan still had to be careful, though. So, we agreed he should hide in the fields and come out only when he heard me whistling a Highland air.

I should have felt happy to

be safe in Queensferry, but instead I was feeling very unhappy. Here I was, all ready to claim my estate of Shaws, but with no idea how I could prove to Mr Rankeillor that I had a right to it.

In my despondency and doubt, I wandered about like a dog that had lost its master. Around nine o'clock, I stopped for a moment to rest outside a fine house with beautiful clear glass windows. Suddenly, the door opened and a kindly looking man came out.

He came up to me.

"What would you be doing here, my lad?" he wanted to know. He sounded sympathetic, so I plucked up courage.

"Could you show me the way to the house of Mr Rankeillor, sir?" I asked.

"Mr Rankeillor, eh?" he said, smiling. "Why, this is the house of Mr Rankeillor." He pointed to the house he had just left and went on: "It's my house!"

What good fortune had brought me to the very house and the very man I sought, I could not imagine.

Mr Rankeillor took me inside, and led me to his study, a dusty little room full of books and documents.

"Now, come to the point,"

he said.

"Very well, sir," I replied. "I have reason to believe myself the rightful heir to the House of Shaws."

"Continue, Mr Balfour," Mr Rankeillor urged. "I must know more about you! Where were you born?"

I told him I was born in Essendean, in 1733. It was the first of many answers I had to give him. Mr Rankeillor questioned me about my father's name, and my mother's, and then wanted to know if I had ever heard of a man called Hoseason.

"I certainly have!" I told him ruefully, and then recounted how my uncle Ebenezer encouraged him to kidnap me and take me to sea, how the ship was wrecked and how I escaped. Mr Rankeillor listened with interest.

"So far," he said, "all you tell me tallies pretty exactly with the information I have about you."

"On the very day you were kidnapped," he went on, "Mr Campbell, the minister of Essendean, came here demanding to know where you were!"

"Your uncle Ebenezer told me he had sent you across to Europe to complete your education. No one really believed him," Mr Rankeillor continued with a smile. "Still, no one could prove anything untoward had happened to you, until Captain Hoseason came to my house and told me that you had drowned. Then, of course, I knew that your uncle was lying!"

It was clear to me now that Mr Rankeillor was a man I could trust. So far, I had breathed not a word about Alan nor of my adventures among the Highlanders, nor of the murder of the Red Fox and the hue and cry afterwards.

"Sir," I told Mr Rankeillor, "if I tell my story, I must ask you to keep it a secret. A friend's life is at stake."

Mr Rankeillor gave me his word. As he listened to me, he leaned back in his chair with his eyes closed. Then, when I mentioned Alan Breck Stewart, he sat up quickly.

"I don't think you should mention the names of any outlaw Highlanders, Mr Balfour," he said seriously. "Perhaps you could just call him your friend?"

So for the rest of my story I called Alan 'Mr Thomson.'

"Well, well," Mr Rankeillor remarked when I had finished. "You have had some great adventures, and your Mr Thomson seems a gentleman of many good qualities."

We broke off then, and Mr Rankeillor led me to a bedroom upstairs where I washed and tidied myself. When I was refreshed, I went downstairs to discover that Mr Rankeillor had an interesting story of his own to tell.

The Trap!

"It started with a love affair," Mr Rankeillor began. "Your father and your uncle Ebenezer fell in love with the same young lady. When she chose your father, Ebenezer nearly went mad with rage. He took to his bed and became quite ill. Your father felt so bad that he offered to give up the lady.

"But she refused to be pushed from one brother to the other as if she were a parcel of goods, and sent them both packing! So, Alexander and Ebenezer fell to bargaining until at last they came to an agreement."

"What agreement was that?" I asked.

"Well, Ebenezer got the estate of Shaws, and your father got the young lady. She was your mother, young David. Because of the bargain, she and your father died poor folk, while Ebenezer got all the land and money."

"But where do I stand in all this?" I wondered.

Mr Rankeillor's reply was

very definite. ''The estate is yours despite the bargain,'' he said. ''Still, if it comes to the law courts, your uncle will fight you and it might even be difficult to prove that he arranged for you to be kidnapped.''

The best thing I could do, according to Mr Rankeillor, was to make a friendly bargain, even if it meant letting my uncle keep the House of Shaws. However, I had a better plan, and one in which both Mr Rankeillor and Alan Breck Stewart had important parts to play. Mr Rankeillor was unwilling, at first, to meet Alan, for Alan was an outlaw and he, as a lawyer, was bound to report such people to the authorities. He solved the problem by deliberately leaving his spectacles behind when we set out, towards evening, to meet up with Alan near his hiding place. This meant, of course, that he could not recognise Alan if he saw him again. As Mr Rankeillor himself put it: ''I am little better than blind without my spectacles.''

Mr Rankeillor's clerk, Mr Torrance, went with us, carrying a special deed which his master had written out.

When we came close to Alan's hiding place, I gave the signal, and Alan stepped out from behind a concealing bush.

Mr Rankeillor approached and I introduced Alan as Mr Thomson.

''Well, sir,'' Mr Rankeillor said to Alan. ''Since you and I are the chief actors in Mr Balfour's plan, I think it a good idea if we walk together to the House of Shaws.''

It was past ten o'clock when we reached the house and, according to plan, Mr Rankeillor, Mr Torrance and I crouched down out of sight while Alan walked boldly up to the front door and began to knock. He made a terrible racket before one of the upstairs windows was thrust up and Uncle Ebenezer poked his head out.

''What d'ye want?'' Uncle Ebenezer croaked, sounding rather frightened. ''I have a blunderbuss here — so take care!''

''Are you Mr Ebenezer Balfour?'' Alan cried, stepping back and looking up into the darkness. ''I have a name for you — David!''

''What was that?'' shrieked Uncle Ebenezer, thoroughly terrified now.

''Do you want me to give you the rest of the name?''

There was a pause. ''I'm thinking I'd better let you in,'' my uncle said in a doubtful tone.

A long time passed before we heard my uncle undoing all the bolts and bars on the front door. At last, there came a creak of the hinges and my uncle appeared on the doorstep, the blunderbuss still in his hands.

"Right now, name your business!" he demanded.

"It's like this," Alan began. "It seems that there was a ship lost not very far from the Isle of Mull, and next day a gentleman of my family came upon a young lad, half-drowned. Well, they brought the lad to his senses and then took him to an old ruined castle, where he remains to this day. The point is this, Mr Balfour: my friends have gone

to some trouble and expense to look after this boy who, or so we are told, was born your nephew. Now, they aren't at all well off and the fact is that unless we come to some agreement about a ransom, you're not likely to see your nephew alive again.''

I heard my uncle clear his throat. ''I don't care much about that,'' he said, at length. ''I'll pay no ransom.''

''Come now, sir,'' Alan went on as if to make my uncle change his mind. ''If this were known you wouldn't be very well thought of hereabouts . . .''

''I'm not very popular here as it is,'' was my uncle's answer. ''In any case, how would anyone know about it? I wouldn't speak of it, and neither would you, nor your friends, wild outlaws that they are!''

''David could tell the story,'' Alan said quietly. ''For if there's no ransom to be paid, they'll just let young David go. Unless, of course, you'd agree to pay my friends for keeping him.''

My uncle made no answer, but began to shift about uneasily. Alan pretended to grow impatient.

''Give me your answer!'' he cried. ''Do you want young David to be killed or kept in prison? Which is it to be?''

''Oh, sir, oh my —'' Uncle Ebenezer started to quaver.

''Killed or kept?'' Alan insisted.

''Keep him, keep him!'' My uncle at last made up his mind. ''I'll have no bloodshed!''

''That'll cost you more,'' Alan told him. ''Killing's easier, quicker and cheaper!''

''No, no, I'd rather he be kept alive,'' returned my uncle. ''If I have to pay for it, well, I'll have to pay.''

''Good,'' said Alan. ''Now about the price. How about the same amount you gave Captain Hoseason for kidnapping the boy?''

''It's a lie, it's a lie!'' my uncle shrieked. ''Kidnapped? David? He never was!''

''Hoseason and I are partners,'' Alan told my uncle. ''You do no good by denying that you paid him, Come now, how much did you give him?''

My uncle hummed and hawed, and then said: ''Twenty pounds. He was going to sell the lad in Carolina as a slave, and get the money back for me.''

Just then, Mr Rankeillor stepped forward out of the darkness. ''Thank you, Mr Thomson,'' he said to Alan. ''Good evening, Mr Balfour,'' he greeted my uncle very politely.

''Good evening, Uncle Ebenezer,'' I said, coming up behind him.

My uncle seemed to be struck dumb. He said never a word, but just stared at us like a man turned to stone. Alan took his blunderbuss and Mr Rankeillor led him back into the house.

"Come, come Mr Balfour," said Mr Rankeillor kindly, as my uncle sat motionless in a chair. "Don't be downhearted, man. We'll come to some easy arrangement over all this."

Torrance was sent to fetch a bottle of wine from the cellar while Mr Rankeillor congratulated me on my good fortune, and Alan upon his excellent performance. Afterwards, we had a good supper while Mr Rankeillor and my uncle sat down to talk in the next room. After an hour, they came out, and my uncle and I set our signatures to the deed of agreement which Torrance had carried in his pocket. It gave me two-thirds of the yearly income of the estate of Shaws.

I was now truly and legally a young man of means, the owner of rich land and property.

In this way, my own story ended happily, but there remained the problem of what to do about Alan. He was still an outlaw, and still had a price on his head for murder.

"You must help your friend get out of the country," Mr Rankeillor told me firmly. "After all Mr Thomson has done for you, it is no more than your duty." Mr Rankeillor was doubtful, though, whether I could help James of the Glens, who, though innocent, was now in prison. "The best you can

do is to make a sworn testimony to his innocence of murder before the judges,'' he advised me. ''I'll give you a letter to the Laird of Pilrig, a much respected man. If you go with him to make your testimony, the judge will pay closer attention to what you say.''

Mr Rankeillor gave me a second letter, this time opening a bank account for me with the British Linen Company. Then, after cautioning me to use my money well, he set out with Mr Torrance to return to Queensferry.

Alan and I turned towards the road that led to Edinburgh. We walked slowly, neither of us having much heart to talk except to settle arrangements for finding a ship that would take Alan safely back to France.

When we came to the hill that overlooked the city of Edinburgh, we both stopped. We both knew without a word being said that we had come to the place where our ways were going to part for ever.

''Well, goodbye,'' Alan said sadly, holding out his hand.

''Goodbye, Alan,'' I said, and giving his hand a brief grasp, went off down the hill.

Neither of us looked each other in the face as we made our farewells. Neither of us looked back for a last glimpse of the other. For both of us were too sad, and too near to tears.